DR. WAYNE W. DYER

with KRISTINA TRACY

It's Not What You've Got!

Lessons for Kids on Money and Abundance

Illustrated by
Stacy Heller Budnick

HAY HOUSE, INC.
Carlsbad, California • London • Sydney
Johannesburg • Vancouver • Hong Kong • New Delhi

Published and distributed in the United States by: Hay House, Inc.: www.hayhouse.com • **Published and distributed in Australia by:** Hay House Australia Pty. Ltd.: www.hayhouse.com.au • **Published and distributed in the United Kingdom by:** Hay House UK, Ltd.: www.hayhouse.co.uk • **Published and distributed in the Republic of South Africa by:** Hay House SA (Pty), Ltd.: orders@psdprom.co.za • www.hayhouse.co.za • **Distributed in Canada by:** Raincoast: www.raincoast.com • **Published in India by:** Hay House Publishers India: www.hayhouse.co.in

Design and Editorial Assistance: Jenny Richards • *Illustrations:* Stacy Heller Budnick

Library of Congress Control Number: 2007920957

ISBN: 978-1-4019-1850-7

10 09 08 07   4 3 2 1
1st edition, September 2007

Printed in Singapore

This Book Belongs to

_____

_____

A Note from Wayne

I have always written and taught that the thoughts and ideas people have about money affect many areas of their lives—their goals, their relationships, and their overall happiness. Developing a healthy view of money at a young age can be invaluable, which is why I felt compelled to write this book. The topics I have included within will help your children build a positive perspective on money, using themes and images they can relate to. By reading this book to your children, you will be giving them a lasting gift.

Wayne W. Dyer

10 Lessons about Money and Abundance for Kids!

#1 You're Not What You've Got!

#2 Live Within Your Means

#3 It Doesn't Matter What "They" Have

#4 You Have the Power to Get What You Want

#5 Money Does Not Create Happiness

#6 Every Job Is Important

#7 Follow Your Own Dreams

#8 There Is Plenty for Everyone, Including You!

#9 You Earned It—Enjoy It!

#10 Abundance Means More Than Money

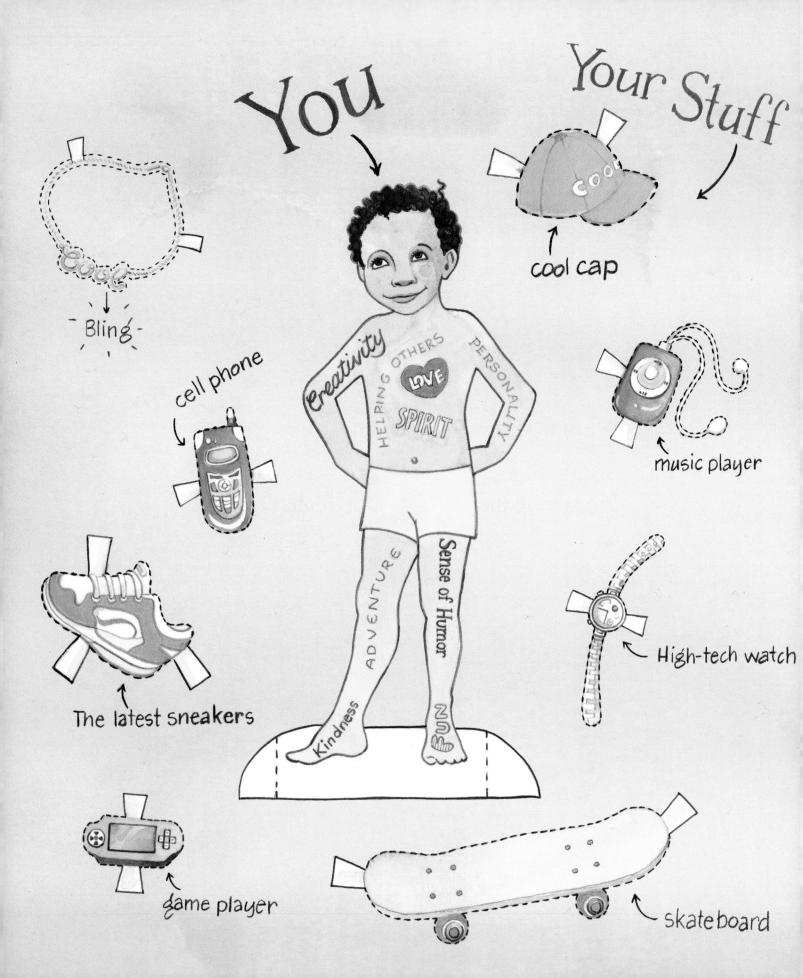

You're Not What You've Got!

Some people think that you are what you've got
and that your toys, clothes, and car really matter a lot.
These things are all fun, there's no denying it's true—
but the things that you own have nothing to do with you.
If you took them away, what would there be?
All the great things about you that are harder to see.

50% OFF SALE
BUY NOW PAY LATER
NO PAYMENTS
UNTIL NEXT YEAR!
SCOOTERS
OPEN
EPIC
X-SCO
EPIC SCOOTERS
X-SCOOTERS

Live Within #2 Your Means

There's an important lesson about money that you should know.
You'll hear it over and over as you grow.
That lesson is: Don't spend more than you make.
Using money that's not yours can be a big mistake.
So while you dream of living large, buy only what you can afford.
Accept what you have at this moment—
the rest you are working toward.

#3 It Doesn't Matter What "They" Have

Some kids have whatever they want, all kinds of fancy stuff.
You might get mad, want what they have, and think you don't have enough.
There will always be people who have more than you, and some who have much less.
Being jealous of what anyone has will get you in a mess.

It's a waste of time and energy to let
these thoughts inside your head.
Turn the page and we will tell you what
to do with your thoughts instead!

You Have the Power #4 to Get What You Want

There's an incredible power that you possess . . .
do you know what it could be?
It's the power of your mind to make something
from nothing—to create your reality.
To make this work and to get what you want,
you must dare to believe,
that wealth and riches of every kind
are something you CAN achieve.
So imagine the things you will do, be, and have—
down to every detail.
Never give up or let others bring you down;
positive thoughts will always prevail.

Money Does Not Create Happiness #5

We live in a world where some people say
that to be happy, having money is the only way.
But you'll never be happy simply because of what you own.
You can have mountains of money and still feel alone.
There are those with little money whose lives are as rich as can be.
They know that the important things are those you can't buy—
they are free!

Every Job #6 Is Important

Some jobs are glamorous, exciting, and fun,
and others are not, but they still need to be done.
Each job is important in its own way—
whether you're the President or shoveling hay.
So when you're on the road to making your dreams come true,
see each job as a blessing, part of what you must do.

Silverhawk

Follow Your #7 Own Dreams

IVY UNIVERSITY GRADS!!

People will ask you, "What do you want to be?"
And you think . . . a dog walker . . . an artist . . . a star on TV. . . .
Some of those you know may try to steer you their way.
They'll say, "This job's much better," or "That job doesn't pay!"
What you do to earn money is your decision to make.
It's your life, so you decide the road that you take.

There Is #8 Plenty for Everyone, Including You!

When others you know have more than you do,
you may start to wonder if there's enough for you.
There's a word called *abundance*—have you heard it before?
It means when it comes to life's gifts, there are always more.
So remember this big word if you're ever in doubt—
and know the great things in life will never run out.

You Earned #9 It—Enjoy It!

When you work hard at a job and do your very best,
you may earn more money than some of the rest.
You can share some of your fortune with others in need—
giving to others is kind and generous, indeed!
But never feel bad that you have what you do—
take pride in your work and the rewards it brings you.

We all know that money
can buy lots of stuff,
but just having money is
not nearly enough.
There are riches to be found
to no end here on Earth.
Your health, great friends—
just think what they're worth.
Love, laughter, and fun,
all these things you can't measure.
And believe it or not . . .
they are the real treasure!

Do you think that having a lot of fancy stuff makes other people think you're cool? What are some things money can't buy that are great about you?

Do you think that your real friends care more about what you have or who you are?

Why do you think it's important to save and use your own money for something you want? How do you feel when you use your own money to buy something?

Have you ever felt jealous when another kid has something you want? Being jealous doesn't feel great—it feels better to enjoy the things you have. What do you have that you're thankful for?

To get what you want in life it helps to picture it clearly in your mind—down to the littlest detail. Describe something you want to do, be, or have. What does it look like? How will you make it happen?

Q u e s t i o n s

Name five things you can buy that make you happy. Now, name five things that make you happy that don't cost money. Although both can make you feel great, it's often the things that are free that bring you happiness that lasts.

What are some types of work that you see people doing every day? Can you see how each job is important? What about the boy shoveling hay—how could that job possibly be important?

There are *so* many jobs to choose from in this world, and other people will have plenty of ideas about which ones are right for you. Why do you think it's so important to choose a job that *you* like?

ABUNDANCE

Do you understand what the word *abundance* means? Does it make you feel good to know that things like love, joy, fun, laughter, and even money will never run out?

Q u e s t i o n s

Every job pays a different amount of money—some more, some less. But no matter how much you make, take pride in the fact that you earned it, and enjoy it. Have you ever made your own money? How did it make you feel?

What is something important that you've learned about money from reading this book? Do you see now how money is not something that is good or bad but will always be a part of your life? Do you understand what money can and can't do? Knowing these answers will help you have a healthy relationship with money throughout your whole life!

Here are some positive thoughts about money and abundance. Understanding these and saying them often to yourself will help make them true for you.

All the best things about me come from within.

I only spend money that I have.

I will create the life that I want.

Every job I do is important.

When I grow up, I will have a job that I love.

The good things in life never run out.

I will always be proud of money that I earn.

I am thankful for every kind of
abundance in my life.

We hope you enjoyed this Hay House book.
If you'd like to receive a free catalog featuring additional Hay House books and products,
or if you'd like information about the Hay Foundation, please contact:

Hay House, Inc.
P.O. Box 5100
Carlsbad, CA 92018-5100

(760) 431-7695 or (800) 654-5126
(760) 431-6948 (fax) or (800) 650-5115 (fax)
www.hayhouse.com® • www.hayfoundation.org

PUBLISHED AND DISTRIBUTED IN AUSTRALIA BY: Hay House Australia Pty. Ltd., 18/36 Ralph St., Alexandria NSW 2015
Phone: 612-9669-4299 • Fax: 612-9669-4144 • www.hayhouse.com.au

PUBLISHED AND DISTRIBUTED IN THE UNITED KINGDOM BY: Hay House UK, Ltd., 292B Kensal Rd., London W10 5BE
Phone: 44-20-8962-1230 • Fax: 44-20-8962-1239 • www.hayhouse.co.uk

PUBLISHED AND DISTRIBUTED IN THE REPUBLIC OF SOUTH AFRICA BY: Hay House SA (Pty), Ltd., P.O. Box 990, Witkoppen 2068
Phone/Fax: 27-11-467-8904 • orders@psdprom.co.za • www.hayhouse.co.za

PUBLISHED IN INDIA BY: Hay House Publishers India, Muskaan Complex, Plot No. 3, B-2, Vasant Kunj, New Delhi 110 070
Phone: 91-11-4176-1620 • Fax: 91-11-4176-1630 • www.hayhouse.co.in

DISTRIBUTED IN CANADA BY: Raincoast, 9050 Shaughnessy St., Vancouver, B.C. V6P 6E5
Phone: (604) 323-7100 • Fax: (604) 323-2600 • www.raincoast.com

Tune in to HayHouseRadio.com® for the best in inspirational talk radio featuring top
Hay House authors! And, sign up via the Hay House USA Website to receive the
Hay House online newsletter and stay informed about what's going on with your
favorite authors. You'll receive bimonthly announcements about Discounts and
Offers, Special Events, Product Highlights, Free Excerpts, Giveaways, and more!
WWW.HAYHOUSE.COM®